Pandemonium

Annette Roberts-Murray

Illustrations by Blueberry Illustrations

I would like to dedicate this book to my granddaughter, Mya Bishop, and my grandson, Chance Bishop, who have helped to inspire me to make this world a better place for all children.

I would also like to dedicate this book to my nephew, Carson McGowan, and my niece, Laila McGowan. I would like to thank Carson for giving me his input and helping me to write this book from a thirteen-year-old boy's perspective.

I would also like to dedicate this book to all of the children around the world who are struggling emotionally and physically to make it through the corona virus pandemic. I encourage you to seek out help if you need someone to talk to. Talk to your parents, a relative, a friend, a pastor, or someone who can help. You do not have to walk this journey alone. There are school counselors and mental health professionals who are available to support you and to help you to make it through these difficult times. We will all make it through this together!

Pandemonium means disorder or confusion and that is what we were experiencing in March of 2020. It was the last day of school, right before spring break was about to begin. Anticipation was in the air as I thought about all the fun things that I wanted to do during the break. Finally, the last bell rang and school was over. I headed to the bus stop to catch my bus home. As I was walking through the campus, I heard kids talking about how the coronavirus had made it to our town. They had been watching the news and they had heard reports on how some people in Montgomery had become sick with the virus. They also had read reports on the internet. I felt afraid. I didn't know how serious this was. I was afraid for myself and my family. I didn't want anyone in my family to get sick. I got on the bus and looked out of the window as the bus drove through the city. After the bus arrived at my stop, I got off and went into the house and asked my mom if she had been watching the news and if she knew that the coronavirus had reached Montgomery. She told me that she had seen the reports. She then assured me that we would be alright.

The next day, I walked into the living room and saw my parents watching the news. They had worried looks on their faces. I asked them what was going on, but they told me that it was nothing for me to worry about. There was a man on the news who was talking about a global pandemic. I didn't know what a global pandemic was at the time, but I soon found out. The man was talking about how the coronavirus was affecting people in different countries. He said that it was also known as COVID-19. I didn't know at that time that the world was about to change drastically.

During spring break, things got worse. We went on lockdown. We couldn't go anywhere, and everyone was being asked to stay at home unless it was an emergency. The stores closed early, and the government put curfews in place to make sure that everyone was inside their homes by a certain time. Everyone began to hoard things such as toilet paper and cleaning supplies because they thought that the stores were going to run out of them. It was pandemonium in the stores. People were not able to get the things they needed because companies could not produce the goods fast enough to meet the demand. We didn't go to the grocery that often because we tried to stay away from large crowds. We always wore our masks and we practiced social distancing whenever we had to go outside.

I couldn't play with my friends, but I talked to them over the phone. Malik was my best friend. We talked a lot over the phone, and we played Xbox online. Malik's father lost his job during the pandemic and it hit his family hard. They struggled to pay their bills. Malik told me that they would take Navy showers to try to conserve water so that their water bill would not be that high. I asked him what Navy showers were and he told me that they were quick showers. Malik's father used to be in the Navy, and he used to take Navy showers. Malik's parents could not afford to pay their phone bill any longer and so Malik's cell phone got cut off. I missed talking to him.

Many of my friends' parents lost their jobs. A lot of them began to worry about how they were going to pay the bills. They were worried that they were going to lose their homes. Many people had to move out of their homes because they could no longer afford to pay their mortgage.

So many people were struggling financially, and there came a time when they couldn't afford to buy food any longer. Some of my friends' parents had to go to the food bank to get food so they could feed their families. Even though some people received unemployment checks, there were many who did not receive any assistance and they struggled throughout the pandemic to try to make ends meet.

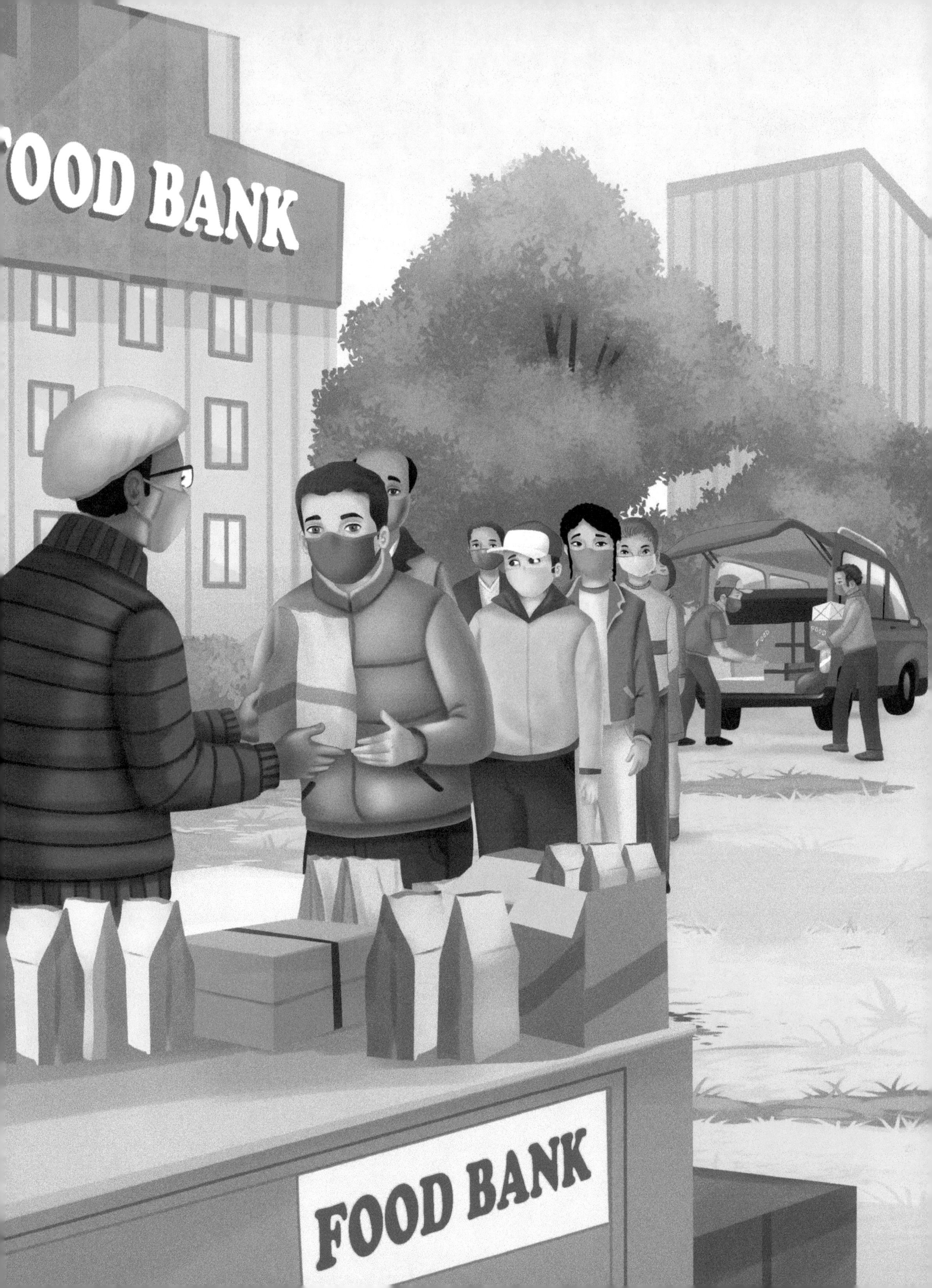
OOD BANK
FOOD BANK

There were a lot of kids in the neighborhood who were struggling emotionally. They couldn't go outside and play with their friends. They were sad to see their parents struggling. It was like a dark cloud hanging over our heads and blocking the sunshine. Some kids were suffering from isolation and depression. I was worried about my family, my friends, and my neighborhood. Things were changing rapidly, and I didn't know how to adjust to the world that was changing right before my eyes. I felt like the air was being sucked out of me.

As the days went by, my parents continued to watch the news for updates on the corona virus. I could tell that they were worried and that made me worry. I was thirteen years old. A thirteen-year-old was not supposed to have to go through a pandemic. At least that's what I thought. I was hoping that this would all be over soon. I wanted the coronavirus to go away. I thought about how I really wanted to go back to school so that I could see my friends again and play in the playground again. I thought about all those times that I complained about getting up in the morning and getting ready for school.

I thought about how I had complained about my school, my teachers, and my classmates, and now I would give anything to go back to school to see my teachers and friends. I longed for a sense of normalcy, but the coronavirus had taken all that away.

The days turned into weeks, the weeks into months, and the months into a year. The coronavirus brought with it quarantine, isolation, social distancing, and boredom. I would often stare out the front window in my living room looking for a sign of life, but I didn't see anyone for a long time. There weren't any kids outside laughing and playing like they used to. Sometimes I would see one or two kids outside, but they were just walking around because they couldn't play with other kids. Even if I went outside, I couldn't play with anyone because we had to stay 6 feet apart. I couldn't go to church anymore because the churches were closed. When spring break was over, we couldn't go back to school because we still had to quarantine. We had to have school online. It was very difficult for me because I needed to be around people. I thrived on social contact.

I watched the news almost every day and it was depressing. I rarely heard about any good news during the pandemic. The news reported about how the hospitals had become overwhelmed with patients and the doctors and nurses were pleading with everyone to stay home and stay safe. I became paranoid. I didn't want to go outside or be around anyone besides my family members. I was afraid to take my mask off because I thought that I was going to get the coronavirus. I was living in fear and I didn't like it. I used to be carefree without a worry and now I found myself worrying about a lot of things. The coronavirus had come in and stolen my safety, security, and peace and I wanted all those things back.

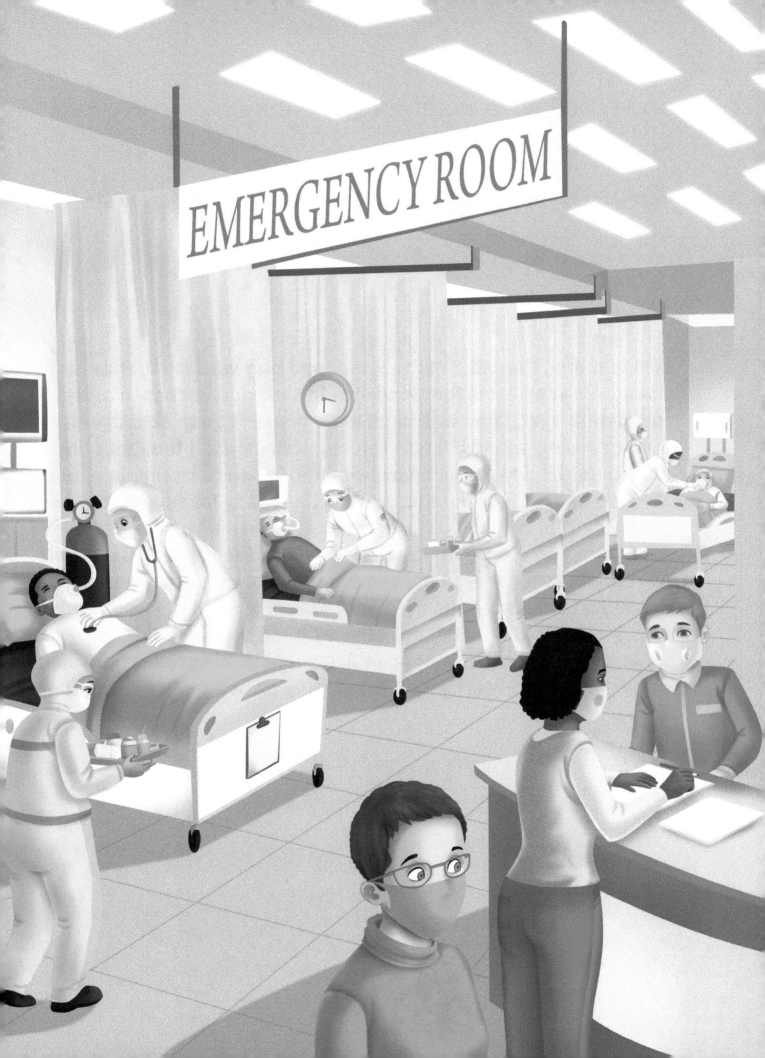

Last summer, I would go to the park and play with my friends, and now, this year, I was forced to stay in the house because of the pandemic. I felt like I was in prison. I couldn't go to school and I couldn't see my friends. It was taking a toll on me. I thought I hated school until it was taken away from me. I used to complain about getting up early in the morning and getting ready for school. I can still hear my mother calling out to me saying, "Carson, you better get out of that bed and start getting ready for school so you won't be late!" Sometimes I would lay in my bed thinking about how I wish I didn't have to go to school. I had friends at school whom I enjoyed playing with. I used to walk to the bus stop with my best friend, Malik. We were in the same class. After school, I would go over to his house and play basketball in his driveway. We used to have a lot of fun together.

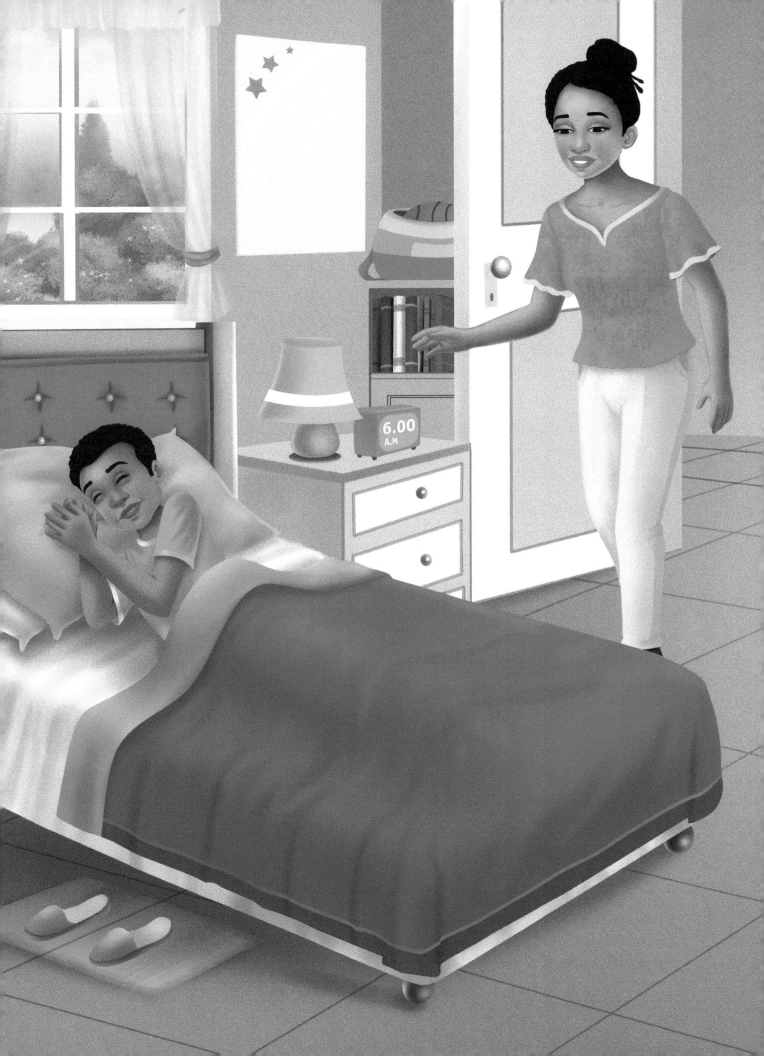

As time went by, things got worse before they got better. Thanksgiving was approaching, but I didn't feel like celebrating the holidays when I knew that so many people were suffering. I also knew that Thanksgiving would be different this year because we couldn't get together and have dinner with the rest of our family members as we had to practice social distancing. I had not seen my cousins or my grandparents in months. It was our family tradition to get together and have dinner during the holidays, but the coronavirus had taken that away. I thought about how we used to sit down at the dinner table and eat all the good food that had been prepared by the women in our family. My grandmother and my aunts used to cook greens, macaroni and cheese, potato salad, deviled eggs, sweet potato pies, deep fried turkey, and pan-baked dressing. The aroma of the food used to spread throughout the house. We would all sit down at the dinner table and hold hands and say grace before we began to eat. There was always loud talking around the dinner table. I missed the smell of the food and the loud conversations that took place at my grandmother's house. This year, my mother cooked Thanksgiving dinner.. It was just the four of us—Mom, Dad, my sister, Laila, and me. She set the food out on the table and we said grace. We then began to talk about all the things that we were thankful for. I was thankful that my family was together and we were all healthy and safe. I was thankful that none of us had the coronavirus. I didn't have a lot of things that I wanted at that time. I had my family, and I was grateful for that.

After Thanksgiving break, we went back to virtual learning. I struggled to keep up and it got harder and harder for me to stay focused. At times, I wanted to give up, but I kept on pushing myself. The weeks went by and I continued to try to do my best to learn online. As Christmas approached, I didn't feel the same anticipation that I had felt in the past. I used to look forward to going on Christmas break and getting Christmas presents, and now it didn't seem to matter to me anymore. I knew that a lot of my friends' parents were not going to be able to afford to buy them gifts this Christmas because they had lost their jobs. How could I think about receiving gifts when there were so many people struggling? There used to be a lot of Christmas parades, but the coronavirus had caused all the parades to be canceled. My mother asked me what I wanted for Christmas. I just wanted the coronavirus to go away so that things could be normal again.

After Christmas break, we were back on the computers participating in distance learning. Scientists all over the world were working hard. There was a race to develop a cure for the coronavirus. They were trying to save people's lives and we were all looking to them to try to save us. One day, I was watching the news and I heard that someone had developed a vaccine for the coronavirus, and they were getting ready to test it to make sure that it would work. I was so excited! Could this finally be over? I wanted to be able to go back to school. I wanted to be able to go over to Malik's house and play basketball with him again. Every day, I watched the news to see if there was any progress being made.

I soon heard that people were participating in trials to test the vaccine. When the vaccine was considered safe, the government began to give it to people. They started to give it to healthcare workers first and then they focused on frontline workers. This included teachers. My mom was a teacher, which meant that she would be able to receive the vaccine early. I was worried. I didn't want her to have any side effects, but I also wanted her to be protected because the government was talking about reopening schools, which meant that she would be exposed to a lot of people. I was hoping that this vaccine would be the cure for the coronavirus. I wanted people to stop dying and I wanted things to be normal again. I wanted to go back to school.

VACCINE

CENTER

I continued washing my hands often and I was constantly cleaning. I wasn't the only one who had become more conscientious of the germs around us. I noticed that my parents were also washing their hands and cleaning the house more often. We did everything we could to try to protect ourselves from the virus. We didn't go out of the house much. It took a toll on us, but eventually we became content with just spending time with each other. During the pandemic, we played a lot of board games and we spent time talking to each other and laughing. We rarely did those things before the pandemic. I guess the pandemic taught us to focus on the things that were truly important. It taught us to spend quality time with each other more and to appreciate each other more. I learned to overlook the small stuff and focus on my love for my family. Instead of getting upset with my sister every time she irritated me, I learned to appreciate her.

During the pandemic, my mother taught me how to cook. I was never really interested in learning how to cook before, but I enjoyed spending quality time with my mother while learning new things. She taught me how to cook chili, spaghetti, and fried chicken. I was proud of myself for learning how to cook. Sometimes, when my parents would come home from work, I would have dinner ready for them and I know they appreciated it. The pandemic had slowly changed me. I was no longer the person I was before the pandemic. It taught me to appreciate so many things that I had previously taken for granted. I learned to appreciate spending quality time with my family members and friends, going to school, going to the movies, and playing sports. As things began to improve and we were able to go outside more often, I found myself wanting to go to the park more, wanting to go to the beach, and just wanting to take in nature. I never really cared about these things before, but now I do. I wanted to live a fuller life now. I learned to pay attention to the things around me that I used to take for granted.

When New Year came, many people celebrated virtually from the comfort of their own homes because social distancing measures were still in place. Just like so many other kids, I suffered from ADD and I had a hard time trying to focus. Distance learning was so difficult and frustrating for me. Sometimes Laila would help me with my homework. She spent a lot of time with me trying to help me understand how to do my math homework. My mother knew I was struggling, and she was very patient with me and I appreciated that. My grades began to drop, and my self-esteem dropped too. I was suffering on the inside and I didn't know what to do. I wondered if things were ever going to get back to normal.

As more and more people began to get vaccinated, the number of coronavirus cases started to decrease. I noticed that many restaurants began to reopen with social distancing measures still in place, and we were finally able to go out to dinner and sit down in a restaurant and eat. We had been getting take-out food for so long that I forgot what it felt like to dine in. I missed being able to go out and do different things, but that was starting to change. We continued to wear our face masks, but we enjoyed seeing people again as so many of them began to come out to restaurants and the movie theater. I was excited to hear that schools would be fully reopening in the fall. I realized that now I was a different person. I went into the pandemic one way, but I came out changed. I didn't think or feel the same way anymore. The things that used to be important to me seemed no longer important. I used to sit in my room for hours and play video games, but during the pandemic, I learned to value spending time with my family. The pandemic taught me to appreciate my life and the people who were in my life. Now I wanted to become a doctor so I could help people.

As the number of coronavirus cases continued to decline, I started to see the light at the end of the tunnel. I was looking forward to a new beginning. I knew that things would never be the same way that they were before the pandemic began because a lot had changed. I didn't want to go back to the way things used to be. I wanted to live in a better world—a world that was filled with love, hope, and peace. The pandemonium was finally coming to an end and I was grateful for that.

Annette Roberts-Murray is an author, wife, mother, and a principal of an elementary school in Stockton, California. She has twin boys named Darius and Demetrius. She also has two grandchildren named Mya and Chance. Annette enjoys working with children. She has worked in the field of education for over 25 years. Annette enjoys helping, supporting, and encouraging children and imagining the possibilities of all that they can become. She enjoys helping others and she is passionate when it comes to advocating for others. Annette also enjoys gardening because she likes to plant seeds and watch them grow. She enjoys talking to her children and grandchildren and spending time with them. Annette has written three books and is currently working on writing a series of children's books. She enjoys traveling to different countries, experiencing new things, and spending time on the beach where she is often seen jet skiing. She has found that the water brings her peace.

CPSIA information can be obtained
at www.ICGtesting.com
Printed in the USA
BVHW021613180122
626539BV00004B/371